W9-CEN-383

Imagination:
THE ART & TECHNIQUE
OF DAVID A. CHERRY

Imagination:
THE ART & TECHNIQUE
OF DAVID A. CHERRY

With Foreword by
Stephen R. Donaldson

THE DONNING COMPANY/PUBLISHERS

Copyright © 1987 by David A. Cherry
Second Printing

All rights reserved, including the right
to reproduce this work in any form
whatsoever without permission in writing
from the publisher, except for brief
passages in connection with a review.
For information, write:

The Donning Company/Publishers
5659 Virginia Beach Boulevard
Norfolk, Virginia 23502

**Library of Congress
Cataloging-in-Publication Data**

Cherry, David A.
   Imagination: the art and technique of
David A. Cherry.

   1. Cherry, David A. 2. Science fiction—
Illustrations. I. Hainer, Beverley B. II.
Reynolds, Kay, 1951-
III. Title.
N6537.C47A4 1987 759.13 87-13411
ISBN 0-89865-564-1
ISBN 0-89865-563-3 (pbk.)

Printed in the United States of America

I dedicate this book with love to the following people, all of whom, in one way or another, have made their contributions: my parents, Basil and Lois; my sister, Carolyn; Bridget Duffield; Real and Muff Musgrave; Hap and Mary Henriksen; Jim and Carol Christensen; Michael and Audrey Whelan; Jim and Janette Gurney; Steve and Stephanie Donaldson; Bob and Pam Adams; Jim and Diane Behring; Roger and Charlotte Rowe; Don Grant; Bill Fawcett; Alex Berman; Don and Elsie Wollheim; Betsy Wollheim and Peter Stampfel; David and Lori Deitrick; Nancy Asire; John Steakley; Kay Reynolds; and of course, Stan and Beverley Hainer and Bob Asprin and Lynn Abbey, who had the faith to envision this book before I did.

Contents

Foreword

David A. Cherry:
Metaphor and Art

I'm probably the only man alive who has the right to make statements like this one: Stephen R. Donaldson is a visual illiterate.

The truth is that I don't *see* with my eyes in any useful aesthetic sense: I *see* with words. Language is my primary perceptual tool.

I don't mean this literally, of course. I'm only illiterate, not blind. My eyes take in visual data just like everyone else's. No, what I mean is that visual data has meaning for me, emotional implication, substantive impact, only when it has been translated into words.

The flip side of this is also true. When I create, I don't start with visual data: I don't *see*. Figuratively as well as literally, the scenes and images in my work exist *because* I describe them. Things come to life *because* I apply language to them: they don't have a life of their own which I struggle to capture in language. For me, words create vision.

All of which raises an interesting question: What the hell am I doing writing an introduction to David A. Cherry's work?

Well, the nice thing about illiteracy is that it can be cured, especially in the young. And the nice thing about people who *see* with words is that they make plausible theoreticians.

For instance: Cherry puts food on his table by being an "illustrator." Much of the work in this very impressive collection was done as "cover art." In other words, the visual images are intended to illustrate—or at least suggest—the contents of the book on which they appear. Here, in the most practical way possible, words create vision. After all, the book isn't written to illustrate the cover art. The book comes first; artists like Cherry labor to *see* the meaning of the words.

So it follows that illustration is a bastard art-form, no? Doesn't true art exist for its own sake? Isn't the work of an illustrator inevitably demeaned by the fact that the ideas don't come from him, but rather from someone else's words?

Oh, yeah?

Illustration, of course, is an honorable calling, with its own history and heroes. Being visually illiterate, however, I'm not burdened with any of that information/tradition/context. Unlike Cherry himself—who finds inspiration in the works of Jean-Leon Gerome (1824-1904) and Laurence Alma-Tadema (1836-1912)—I *see* with language; and what I *see* when I look at good illustration is William Blake.

Blake (1757-1827) was a brilliant and eccentric English poet who illustrated his own work with brilliant and eccentric art—art which often bears no particularly obvious relationship to the poetry. As an illustrator, he couldn't get it right. What he saw didn't match what he wrote—or vice versa. And yet he clearly intended one to illustrate the other.

As I said, eccentric.

I didn't bring him up because he was eccentric, however, but because he was brilliant. Nearly 150 years after Blake's death, theoreticians began to understand the relationship between his poetry and his art (ref. the seminal work of Dr. Harold Hower in this field); and that understanding sheds light on both, language and vision.

I'll try to be clear about this. Writing (like music) is an organization of *time*: it is linear; words must be placed one after the other in order to make sense; to be comprehended, words must be perceived *in sequence*. Painting, on the other hand, is an organization of *space*: all the elements of a painting present themselves simultaneously to the eye; comprehension involves the perception of shape, color, texture rather than of sequence. Writing relys on memory, the ability to retain the meaning of one word while reading the next. Painting relys on—what? This is where we visual illiterates get into trouble. On the ability, perhaps, to see the relationships between details instantly, as a whole, rather than over time; relationships which exist—drawing a rather strained analogy from geometry—only in three dimensions, not in two.

Well, what is any medium of communication good for? Metaphor, that's what. Metaphor is what allows any medium of communication to transcend itself, to go beyond, for example, arbitrary sounds, arbitrary black squiggles on paper, into the realm of passion and insight. And what is metaphor? Literally, it is a comparison based on the similarity between unlike things—based, in practice, on the communicator's ability to inspire a leap of imagination in the communicatee. Hence, metaphor is the means by which creators are able to communicate things which are figuratively true but literally impossible.

To boldly go where no mere exposition has gone before.

Sorry about that.

(The point, Donaldson. Get to the point.)

Theoreticians began to understand Blake when they began to grasp the nature of metaphor. Writing, being an organization of *time*, is especially good at expressing metaphors of *space*. ("The similarity between unlike things.") Painting, on the other hand, being an organization of *space*, is especially good at expressing metaphors of *time*. That's the basis on which Blake's poetry and art illustrate each other. And it's the basis on which we visual illiterates can understand what makes an artist like David Cherry so good.

In a book, the motion of time is taken for granted: seconds pass as the words tick by; sequences of action split or converge. Time is memorable only if the words are dull. Who did what to whom in what order is such a mundane consideration that many writers pay no attention to it—with no loss to the excitement or vividness of their work. But the visual images which leap into the reader's mind are another matter. Starscapes, space stations, the curve of the deck, Kif and Hani faces: these things have emotional implication, substantive impact, precisely because they are metaphorical.

And they are precisely the things which illustration takes for granted. Cherry knocks out that stuff as a matter of course. His art for Brin's *Startide Rising* is a good example because it's subtle. There's the spaceship, there's the starscape, there's the planet. And so what? Ah, but the ship is *moving*. It can't, obviously. A painting is an organization of *space*. Movement requires *time*. But the metaphor—The ship is *moving*, traversing time as well as distance; and so the illustration conveys a sense of secret importance, almost of haste; a sense of destination. Because Cherry is able to suggest that the ship is *moving* (a metaphor of time), he can communicate excitements and possibilities which Brin with all his talent can only approximate.

Another way to make the same point is to say that each of Cherry's illustrations contains a compressed story, an implied sequence of events and emotions, a literally impossible movement from here to there. And that story, that sequence, that movement is no bastard achievement because it doesn't come from the book, the writer. It can't: the book is an organization of time and can only make numinous the materials which illustration takes for granted. No, what real art of all kinds does is transcend itself through metaphor.

And that is what Cherry's work does here.

Metaphors of time: the concept is a potential cure for visual illiteracy.

STEPHEN R. DONALDSON

Introduction

Stanley Hainer

The Offering by David Cherry is one of my most prized possessions and it occupies a special place in a special room in my home.

To see its development grace the pages of the technique section of this book is an added pleasure and it gives all of us the opportunity to look over David's shoulder as he captures an idea and, with thought and care, brings it to fruition.

The diversity of art included here ranges from covers of books to images of friends, yet each piece reflects that combination of sensitivity and humor, intellect and imagination, which culminate in David the man and David the artist.

Publishing always provides excitement, often pride, and occasionally pleasure. Rarely are all three of these feelings embodied in the publication of one book. *Imagination: The Art and Technique of David A. Cherry* achieves that special status.

Excitement and wonder fill each page. Enjoy them all.

Stanley Hainer
Vice President
Donning Publishing Co.

Preface

Imagination. If there is hope for a good tomorrow, where is it but in our imagination? When our minds give birth to our most wondrous, hopeful thoughts, how do we communicate them to our friends? We say, "Just imagine...," and our eyes gleam in delight at our dreams.

We long to see behind the curtain of the possible. Our minds reach out to examine new alternatives, to touch and explore the unattainable. In such ways our fancies have led inexorably to achievement upon achievement over the centuries.

And in each man's personal progress, where does he look to understand what is best in mankind, what he should be and can be if he will? It is in the world's myths, legends, and fantasies that we have stored our most telling examinations of such basics as love, beauty, courage, nobility, compassion, and self-sacrifice.

As an artist, I have no desire to spend my talents in a glorification of the mundane or commonplace. If I am to communicate visually, I want to take you to places past, future, and neverwhen, let you walk the streets of ancient Rome, strap in for a tour of the galaxy, or sit on a single leaf and see the world through the eyes of a pixie. I want to express the positive lessons of myth and fantasy in forms which strengthen as they entertain.

It is little wonder, then, that I have come to spend so much of my time illustrating works of science fiction and fantasy. The authors of these stories are the creators of new myths, legends, and fancies to rival those of Greece and Rome. They keep alive our sense of wonder, our sense of the possible, and look forward to alternatives other than nuclear winter or gradual stagnation. I enjoy being a part of that.

Yet I am not wholly an illustrator. I have my own stories to tell and fantasies to share. These I set down in works purely my own.

It is in hope that you may find some enjoyment in them that I have brought together my illustrations and other works in this book. And in hope that some of the technical knowledge I have been able to piece together will be of assistance to aspiring artists, I have included a specific section on technique.

So take a deep breath, allow yourself to believe for a while that anything is possible, and join me in the realms of fantasy and imagination.

Techniques

I must begin by stating plainly that I do not claim to know the *right* way to draw or paint. At most, I know how I might approach a given subject or problem. That is what I offer here.

While my subject matter usually deals with the fantastic or romantic, I am essentially a realist in style. Again, this is not necessarily *right* or *best*. It is what I prefer. You may prefer to express yourself in an entirely different style. But I believe that if you learn the disciplines necessary to achieve realism, you will be able to apply them to any style which suits your expression.

I work chiefly in acrylics, although I do often make use of oil paints for certain effects and finishwork. In order to illustrate my approach, I have taken a series of photographs detailing the progress of a single painting from its initial concept to its completion and will examine them in sequence. Non-artists may find it interesting to see what actually goes into a painting. Experienced artists may get a giggle out of it. Hopefully, up-and-coming artists will find something useful.

Before delving into strictly technical areas, I would like to say a word or two of a more general nature. My best advice to beginning artists is to take it one step at a time and be ready to work long hours for a little progress.

Start with what you already do best. Hone that to razor sharpness in painting after painting. But keep it simple. Do not let your love of the subject matter overcome your interest in improving your technique. The best subject poorly executed still results in a poor painting.

And be self-critical. Don't cheat yourself with complacency. "Good enough" and "close enough" usually aren't. But always remember too, while the cup may be only half full, it is never half empty, and you will learn more from your failures than your successes.

With that caveat in mind, we may move on to consider technique *per se*.

Drawing skills come first. The colors you use as you paint are far less important than use of light and dark. Your sketch is where you work out all your problems and relative lights and darks.

As a novice, I drew totally from my imagination and thought I had a useable sketch once I had a reasonable line outline of the object I wanted to paint. I figured the interior shadings would suggest themselves as I began to apply paint. Too often, my object when painted looked stiff, out of proportion, out of perspective, flat, or any combination thereof. A good friend suggested that until I had acquired the experience of Michelangelo, I should draw from life or other adequate reference rather than try to rely solely upon my imagination. He also impressed upon me the necessity of working out my interior shadings at the drawing stage.

Trust me. Your work *will* go faster and be better in the long run if you take the time at the start to work out your interior shadings while you are still dealing with the blessed simplicity of a monochrome sketch. And drawing from live models or good photographic reference will help eliminate problems in proportion and perspective.

Some artists will tell you to draw only from life and insist that photo references are a cheat and lead to stiff figures. I prefer to use both, and I think photo reference, used properly, can be an invaluable tool for the novice as well as the master. While both life drawing and photo reference teach proportion and perspective, the advantage to life drawing is that it also helps you catch the essential gesture of a figure and avoid stiffness. The disadvantage for the novice is that you rarely have time to note all the nuances of shading which control whether the resulting painting will appear dimensional or flat. Photo reference allows time to examine all the subtle values within each shadow or highlight, but it is tempting to rely on photos too much. Do not simply trace from them. Treat them like a live model and draw from them.

As an exercise (to be interspersed with continuing practice at life drawing), I would suggest that you occasionally take a good 8 x 10 photo of a subject and, in pencil, recreate each shading as minutely and exactly as possible. In pushing yourself to draw to exact reality this way, you will find there is far more to record than you had previously noticed. Later, you will find it easier when you have to work out shadings from imagination alone. More important still, you will find that being able to achieve

photographic reality if you choose, allows you to approach it as closely or as distantly as is necessary for the effect you want and gives you greater latitude in your artistic expression.

Figure No. 1 of the illustrations for this section is my sketch for the cover painting of this book. In this instance, I was drawing totally from my imagination, but I did not rely on a simple outline of my figure. I worked out the value of each shadow and highlight in relation to the whole. Having done it once in monochrome, I knew almost exactly the values I wanted to achieve with my paint and eliminated a great deal of trial and error at that stage.

I shade in pencil in the same way I paint—in layers. Working one small section at a time, I lay down a shade, create interior highlights with a kneaded eraser, soften edges with my finger or a paper stub, and add interior textures with pencil point or side, as appropriate. Then I use these same procedures over again as often as necessary to adjust the lights and darks to suit me before I move on to the next section. When all sections are finished, I go over the drawing again as a whole, making sure that each section fits in unity with the whole.

I still do this fairly poorly. If you want to see pencil shading done properly, take a look at the work of someone such as Dell Harris, respected fantasy artist and fellow Oklahoman. I credit Dell with anything I do right in drawing. The mistakes are my own doing.

With a finished sketch in hand to serve as a road map for the painting, the next consideration is the preparation of the board or canvas. I prefer a relatively untextured surface with a fair degree of porosity. I therefore use illustration board or masonite and greatly prefer the latter. Tempered masonite is not suitable since it has oil heat-rolled into its surface. Accordingly, I use untempered masonite (as shown in Figure No. 2) which has no oil on its surface.

Once cut to size, the board should be very lightly sanded, just enough to break the surface. Next, I apply acrylic gesso to the

Figure No. 1—*The sketch is the road map for values of light and dark. The pencil shading is done in layers.*

Figure No. 2—*The untempered masonite board is lightly sanded, just enough to break the surface.*

board. I use a *dry* No. 12 flat white bristle brush with just enough gesso on it to cover an area a little larger than a silver dollar at one time. I do not paint it on. I scrub it in, working quickly to spread it evenly before it dries. The object is to avoid having any actual brush strokes to sand away later. Do not panic if the first coat looks too thin to you. After three or four coats of gesso, sanding *very* lightly between coats, the result will be a smooth but lightly toothed surface much like that of cold pressed illustration board (see Figure No. 3). I find any time spent applying gesso this way is worth it for the type of surface I achieve. Besides, it is usually compensated by time saved in sanding.

With the board prepared, my next step, in the case of this painting, was to paint in the background. Whenever possible, I prefer to paint my background completely before I add the figures and foreground elements. This avoids unsightly edges around the figures.

In this situation, I chose a simple textured background reminiscent of stone. To achieve

it, I again resorted to my No. 12 flat bristle brush. Holding it like a dagger with the bristles pointing down, I immersed it in a very wet puddle of acrylic paint and water then jabbed it up and down over the surface of the board. The bristles spreading out and then popping up made bubbles on the wet surface. The paint, suspended in the water, collected most thickly at the bubbles. I then partially dried the surface with a hairdryer. This dried the areas of thin suspension between the bubbles and turned the bubbles to dark puddles. Some puddles I let dry entirely to form solid spots and shapes. Others I let dry only around the edges, blotting up their centers with tissue to leave rings and swirls. Color upon color, layer upon layer, I repeated the process until I was pleased with the result.

Next, it was time to transfer my drawing from the sketch pad to the surface of my board. Fortunately, I had had the foresight to make my sketch the exact size of the image I wanted to paint. So, I placed tracing paper

17

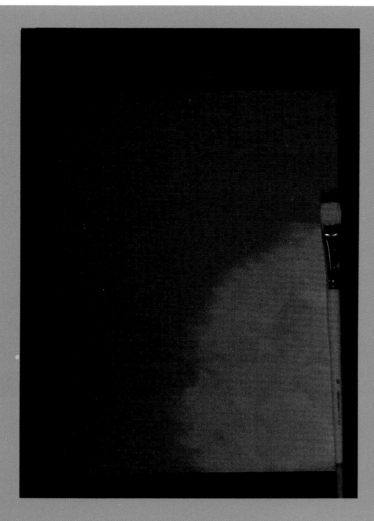

Figure No. 3—Gesso is scrubbed on with a dry brush to achieve a slightly toothed surface with no actual brushstrokes.

Figure No. 4—Outlines of each major element of the sketch are traced onto tracing paper. The outlines are then retraced on the backside of the paper.

over the sketch and traced the outlines of each element of the drawing (see Figure No. 4). I then turned the tracing over, retraced it in soft lead on the back, flipped it rightside up again, taped it to my painting surface, and used a burnisher (in this case nothing more than a ball point pen which had run out of ink) to impress the lines onto the board. I was careful to transfer only the outside lines of the major elements, leaving interior lines to be transferred at a later stage.

Instead of carefully retracing the lines on the back of the tracing paper as I do, you may cover the whole back of the tracing paper with graphite (using the side of your pencil) or you may simply lay a piece of commercially prepared transfer paper under your tracing. I still prefer the first method because it lets me see more of the painting through the tracing paper and keep track of what I have traced

and what I have not.

If my sketch had not been the right size to start with, I would have used an opaque projector to enlarge or reduce it to correct size, and then I would have traced from the projection.

With an initial outline of the figure on the board, the next step is to begin the actual painting. As shown in Figure No. 5, I started filling in each major section of the outline with a flat tone of medium value in colors appropriate to provide a base for each section. For the skin tones, I chose a greyed white mixed with burnt sienna. For areas which would eventually be folds of white cloth, I chose a light blue since I wanted the cloth to have a cool blue tint in contrast to the warm colors in the rest of the painting.

In Figure No. 6, I continued painting base colors, some thickly as in the collar and torso

Figure No. 5—Outlines of major elements are burnished from the tracing to the board and painted in flat base tones of medium value.

Figure No. 6—Interior detail from the tracing is transferred onto the areas of flat base tone.

where I wanted a solid base, and others thinly as in the feathers and fur where the streakiness of my brush strokes would aid in the illusion I was seeking. Note the warm red oxide of the collar to serve as a base for an illusion of brass or gold and to contrast directly with the blued cloth next to it. You can also see in Figure No. 6 that I have resorted to my tracing again and burnished in some of the interior lines of the face, hands, torso, horns, and cloth. In the blued areas, I have even painted in some of the lines denoting shadows. And on a portion of the figure's left sleeve, I have begun to add shading.

In Figure No. 7, I have begun to play with shadings throughout the figure. Although I only use water with my acrylics and do not use any gels, mediums, or extenders, the primary technique used in shading is ana-

logous to the use of glazes in oil painting. I simply suspend the paint in enough water to make it merely tint the area I am painting. Of course, transparent colors work very well for this, but even opaque colors can be applied to let the base color shine through if sufficiently suspended in water.

I do not first dampen the area I am trying to glaze as one might in watercolor technique. To do so would cause previously glazed areas to *pick up* as I attempt to brush on additional layers. To further guard against disturbing one layer of glaze while putting on another, I usually warm the area with a hairdryer after each layer to *set* or harden the glaze. When this is done, the layers of glaze are remarkably resistant to disturbance. You would have to actually scrub them with a stiff, damp brush to bother them.

While it is generally true that acrylics dry

19

Figure No. 7—Shading is applied in layered glazes which can be blended somewhat with the soft, damp stub of a worn out brush.

Figure No. 8—Interior darks and highlights are added to glazed areas and glazed again, the process repeated as necessary.

too fast to be blended directly on the board, the fact that you *can* pick up layered glazes, move them around, or blend them with a stiff, damp brush and a little scrubbing provides a very useful exception to this rule. When my brushes wear down to a short, soft stub, I keep them around for just this purpose. You can get some slick blends and great softened edges with this trick. Of course you have to be careful or you will scrub right back down to the gesso and have to start all over again.

The general idea in glazing is to start with your base color (which, as you will recall, is a medium value), glaze it down to a desired darkness (in whole and/or in interior sections), opaquely or translucently paint in any interior darks, paint or glaze in your highlights, and then keep repeating the process until the desired gradations of light and dark

are achieved.

As an example, I painted in the lights and darks of each interior diamond on the torso in Figure No. 7 with translucent lights and darks (yellowed grey for the highlights and burnt umber with an upper border of burnt sienna for the darks). Then to round the torso as a whole, I glazed it with a suspension of burnt sienna followed by several glazes of hooker's green around the edges of the shoulders and torso. Following this, I again adjusted the individual highlights and darks of the interior diamond shapes. As can be seen in subsequent photos, I kept repeating the process until I had a satisfactory three-dimensional effect.

In Figure No. 8, I continued to play with shadings, glazing things darker, adding their highlights, painting opaque deeper darks, adding highlights within highlights, glazing

20

Figure No. 9—Shadings are constantly adjusted throughout to match the values established in the monochrome sketch.

Figure No. 10—Jewels are easy: a base dark, bordered with a white highlight and a splash of color.

the whole darker again, over and over. I also began to shade in the features of the face, arms, and hands. Normally I would work a good deal of shading into the face, but I decided at this point to keep it looking fairly flat and oval to remain consistent with the design of the figure as a whole, almost every element of which was based on circles or ovals.

In Figure No. 9, I transferred the placements of pearls and jewels from my tracing to the board and began to paint them in. Jewels give such a tremendously dimensional effect for so little effort that I tend to think of them as a cheap trick: a base dark, bordered with a white highlight and a splash of color, and you have a jewel. But the joke was on me this time when I wound up having to work out the relative brilliance of each little pearl. That kept me busy for quite a while.

In Figures No. 10 and 11, I was still mostly playing with the jewels, although I distracted myself from that tedium by adjusting lights and darks throughout the figure whenever my eye noticed anything distracting. Most notably in Figure No. 11, I glazed in colors and tones on the shells around the lady's face, almost finished the areas of blued cloth, added form to the skirt, and began to paint in (very thinly) the fur wrap.

In Figure No. 12, there was little left to do, but that is always where whatever you decide to do becomes very important. I continued adjusting lights and darks throughout the figure. Most notably, however, I used oil paints to finish up the face as well as parts of the hands and arms. I did this because I wanted more smoothly gradated tones on the lady's flesh than I had achieved even with glazes of acrylic.

21

Figure No. 11—Values of light and dark are still adjusted. Color is a secondary consideration.

Figure No. 12—Skin tones are overpainted in oils to achieve even softer blends of color and value.

If I had wanted to stay with acrylics, I could have tried to use my airbrush, but I judged the area too small for my meager talents with it. Besides, I *hate* friskets (little masks cut to block out areas you do not want to paint). I could also have continued glazing and blending glazes with that little trick I mentioned earlier using a dampened stub of a brush. All in all, though, oils seemed best suited for the effect I wanted.

I find acrylics best for some effects, oils best for others, and I do not hesitate to use both in a painting, although I am careful to put on oils last and not to get them on any areas which I eventually want to cover with acrylic. (If you paint acrylics over oils, they will just peel off.) Some of the oldest and best preserved paintings in existence were oils on board over an egg tempera underpainting. I see no reason not to use acrylic in place of

egg tempera, but then I see no reason to overpaint in oils where I am already satisfied with the effect of my acrylic.

The one problem painting partly in acrylic and partly in oil over acrylic might cause is a disparate yellowing or aging of the oils compared to the acrylics. The acrylics would remain bright much longer than the oils. To eliminate this problem, there being no way to make the oils stay bright as long as the acrylics, I simply assure that the acrylics will appear to age at the same rate as the oils. To do this I coat the finished painting with clear oil painting medium, let that dry, and then apply a varnish such as dammar. Effectively, this makes the entire surface of the painting an oil painting even though the viewer is, for the most part, merely looking through the clear oil to the acrylic work beneath. All in all, a painting finished in this fashion should, if

Figure No. 13—The finished product—painting the figure over a finished background has added to the dimensional effect.

done on masonite, last for an incredibly long time and age evenly.

Since my digression on the merits of acrylics versus oil paints was occasioned by my need for a smooth gradation of flesh tones, I feel it proper to disgress further to cover a question often asked by beginning artists, that being, "What colors do you use for flesh?" The only true answer is, "It varies."

In the painting at hand, my base color for the flesh was, as stated previously, a light neutral grey mixed with burnt sienna. Straight burnt sienna formed most of the shading, with burnt umber blended in for the darkest tones. Highlights were formed, not with white (which makes a face go pasty), but rather with yellows and yellowed whites or yellowed light greys. I went through the entire process from start to

finish once in acrylic and once in oils, applying the oils rather like cosmetics with Liquin as my medium so they would dry overnight.

In this painting I did not require any serious blue or grey tints to the skin tones. Still, I might mention that one interesting trick of several of the old masters was to underpaint flesh in a monochrome of ivory black and white, then overpaint in flesh tones. Many of the subtle "blue" shadings in such areas as the corner of a mouth on fine old paintings were achieved merely by allowing the monochrome grey underpainting to show through sufficiently at given points.

All this is well and good as far as it goes, but I must stress that there is no magic formula for flesh tones. You can paint a person green, red, blue or—any other color—and still have the skin look like flesh. Think about it.

What makes flesh look like flesh, or any object look like what it is supposed to be, is the way we perceive light reflecting from it. The gradation of light and dark and the relative intensities of highlights and shadows are the most important aspects of painting any object or figure. Get those right and you are in business. Get them wrong and your painting is flat and lifeless. Either way, color does not do all that much to help. It is purely a secondary consideration.

Why do you think so many of the old masters underpainted in a grey monotone? Just to get "blue" tones at the corner of a mouth? Think again.

Finally we come to Figure No. 13. I may have added a touch or two of paint after this picture was taken, but it shows what is essentially the finished work. Since Figure No. 12, the only identifiably major work has been on the fur, but again, I was scouring the figure over and over, searching for minute adjustments in the shadings, always with an eye to the overall balance.

I always find it hard to consider any painting as finished. If I look hard enough and long enough, I know I will find more things to adjust and correct. Still, there comes a time when I am either so sick of looking at the darned thing that I am ready

Technique

to throw it across the room or I find that I have been sitting and staring at it for hours without finding anything to adjust which I know *how* to adjust. Then too, if the painting is an illustration, sometimes the deadline comes, ready or not. This, however, was one of those nice paintings which just said, "It's OK. You can stop now. I'm finished." And so it was.

Before leaving this section on technique, I thought it would be appropriate to have a look at my work station. I work at a drafting table. I can't stand easels. Figure No. 14 shows an aerial view of my setup for acrylics. It is a cookie sheet. At the top right is a container of water. At the bottom is a soaked paper towel with paints on it in little piles. I mix either in the middle of the cookie sheet or in the depressions of the little tray which appears at top left. Once or twice during the day, I add a little water to the paper towel. At the end of the day, I put the whole arrangement into an airtight plastic container. This way my paints stay moist and usable for a week or two at a time.

Figure No. 15 is a photo of my brushes. I use a lot of 0's, 1's, and 2's, mostly rounds, and mostly synthetic bristles. The stubby red round one extending bottommost in the photo is primarily useful to me as a blender brush in oil-painting small areas, but it can also be helpful in some acrylic glazing and even acrylic "dry" brush techniques.

Figure No. 16 shows my setup for oil painting. It is just a scrap piece of mat board covered with aluminum foil. Although I can use one or two brushes for an entire acrylic painting, it takes a number of brushes at one time to do an oil painting. For each color (and often for each shade of color) I dedicate a set of two brushes: one medium length round to apply the paint and one short soft-bristled brush to blend the color or shade into the surrounding paint. I start with the brushes

Figure No. 14—*My setup for acrylics: water, brushes, a cookie sheet and a paper towel.*

dry and do not allow them to touch thinner until I am through for the day and ready to clean them. If one becomes too contaminated with the wrong shade, I set it aside and replace it with a new one.

Well, there you have it: most of what I know on the subject of technique. As I said, it may not be anyone's idea of the *right* way to paint, but it works just fine for me. I hope you have found some things in it which will work well for you too.

Figure No. 15—My brushes are mostly 0's, 1's, and 2's, mostly rounds, and mostly synthetic.

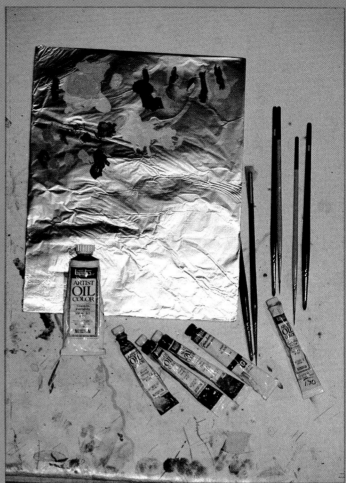

Figure No. 16—My setup for oils: tinfoil on matboard and a set of brushes for each tone.

Fantasy Art

The Summoning

Cover painting for Ealdwood *by C. J. Cherryh, published by Donald M. Grant, West Kingston, Rhode Island. Pen and watercolor on illustration board. Copyright© 1980 by David A. Cherry.*

I have not held strictly to any order of presentation in this book, but I thought it would be nice to begin at the beginning. *The Summoning* is my first published work and has a special place in my affection.

I illustrated *Ealdwood* as a bit of a lark while still a full-time attorney. Its illustrations along with one other painting mark the only two times my sister and I actively sought the chance to work together as author and artist, although we have been fortunate to have others present us with that opportunity from time to time since then.

When I applied to Donald Grant to do the art for *Ealdwood,* I did not believe he would agree to let me do the project, and I thought he would want pen and ink drawings. To my surprise, he not only agreed to let me do the work but wanted several color works. I did them with a fine tipped ball point pen and a cheap set of hastily acquired watercolors, learning as I went.

In my soul, I wanted to work as a realist, but I was so far from having the skills for that that I was very nervous about letting the illustrations in *Ealdwood* see the light of day. Still, there is some elemental quality in them that I love and feel I have missed in some far more polished works done later on.

Gift of Eald

Interior illustration for Ealdwood *by
C. J. Cherryh, published by Donald M. Grant,
West Kingston, Rhode Island. Pen and watercolor
on illustration board. Copyright© 1980 by
David A. Cherry. In the collection of Danille
and Steven Monson.*

Gift of Eald is one of the six interior illustrations of *Ealdwood*. It shows the elf, Arafel, casting a glamor over a flower to amuse a small human child. As you can see, the works from *Ealdwood* are actually painted drawings. I had not really had much experience with paints prior to this project. That is why I chose to work with pen and watercolor. That combination of media allowed me to simply stain the color over my drawings. I chose to use a common ball point pen because it was the only pen and ink source familiar to me at the time which would not run or smear when I went over it with water and paint.

I do not know for certain whether I would eventually have turned to art as my career had I not become involved in the art for *Ealdwood*. I like to think I would have, but I do know that doing the *Ealdwood* project forced me for the first time to approach art with the same serious concentration and dedication I had previously reserved for legal studies. I became intrigued with how much more there was to be learned. Having opened that door, I realized that, whether I continued law or not, I could never again *not* paint.

It was only a couple of years after finishing *Ealdwood* that I made up my mind to seek a career in art. Given my level of skill at the time, I knew the decision was presumptuous, perhaps foolhardy. But if I had learned anything from my studies in classical culture and law, it was how to learn. I was confident of that and my willingness to work hard. I have never regretted my choice.

The Sentry

Acrylic on illustration board. Copyright © 1982 by David A. Cherry. In the collection of Winton E. Matthews, Jr.

The Sentry is one of a short series of fairy paintings done early on in my exploration of acrylic painting techniques. I am as pragmatic a businessman as you would care to meet, but I feel sorry for small, insecure minds that have lost all the wonder and goodness of that which is child*like* in their eagerness to avoid that which may seem child*ish*. As a young boy, I avidly read the tales of "Mary Jane and Sniffles" in the back of my Warner Bros. comics. Mary Jane was a pretty little girl, and Sniffles was her best friend, a little mouse in a blue suit. Mary Jane would sprinkle herself with pixie dust and recite the magic words:

> "Now I close my eyes real tight,
> And I wish with all my might!
> Magic words of poof, poof, piffles,
> Make me just as small as Sniffles!"

Then she and Sniffles would wander through her garden having marvelous adventures with the animals and insects who lived there.

I recall sitting in my sand box throwing sand up like pixie dust and saying the magic words. I never did become as small as Sniffles, but I can't say that the magic didn't work. In my mind my garden became a fantastic playground. I never really outgrew the wonderful images of being small enough to climb a zinnia like a palm tree or gaze into a water droplet as large as a crystal ball. Imaginings such as these are a treasure to be nurtured for a lifetime, not just in childhood.

Arafel (Study in Green)

Acrylic on masonite. Copyright© 1982 by David A. Cherry. In the collection of Lenore Jean Jones.

The second and last time I ever tracked down an opportunity to illustrate one of my sister's stories was when Don Wollheim of DAW Books had invited her to expand the novella, *Ealdwood*, into the novel which eventually became *The Dreamstone*. Having drawn the main character, Arafel, my way in the special edition of *Ealdwood*, which saw only limited distribution, I did not relish the idea of her being presented to the majority of the reading public through the eyes of another artist on the cover of the mass-market paperback. Admittedly, this attitude was hardly professional, but then neither was I at the time, and after working so very hard over *Ealdwood*, I felt very proprietary about Arafel.

In any event, knowing approximately when Carolyn would be sending in her manuscript of the novel, I contrived to follow it shortly with this painting, along with a note apologizing for submitting an unsolicited cover painting. Happily, the people of DAW Books liked it and gave me the cover assignment, with one exception. They wanted it in something other than green.

Don Wollheim explained to me that green covers tend to fade on the shelves faster than other colors; that green covers tend to sell fewer copies of a book; and that while a book may describe its cover scene as being bathed in green light, the primary function of a cover painting, apart from being an illustration, is to serve as a poster to attract the eye and promote sales. It was good advice which I have always valued. Still, I have a fondness for the original green version of *Arafel* and wanted the opportunity to let you see it here.

Arafel

Cover painting for **The Dreamstone** *by
C. J. Cherryh, published by DAW Books, Inc.,
New York, New York. Acrylic on masonite.
Copyright© 1982 by David A. Cherry. In the
collection of C. J. Cherryh.*

This is *Arafel* as it finally appeared on the
DAW Books edition of *The Dreamstone*. You
may notice that the sword is longer here than
it appears on the cover. It was interfering
with the type on the book title (or vice versa),
so some kind soul painted over the portion
of the sword they didn't want with watercolor. When the painting was returned, I had
to carefully remove the watercolor and
repaint that section.

The main background color of both this
and the green version on the previous page
were laid in with an airbrush. I did not,
however, have a fine enough touch with an
airbrush to handle the detail work on the
clouds, and I chose not to attempt it with
regular brush work. Instead, I bought nine or
ten different types of erasers and set to work
meticulously wearing away the background
colors to allow the white gesso ground
beneath to show in varying degrees. It was
only because the paint had been sprayed on
so evenly in loose layers that the erasing
technique worked as smoothly as it did. If I
had brushed the paint on to start with,
erasing would never have worked. As it was,
it took hours and hours of delicate work, but
the result was worth it. I do recall, however,
upon learning I would have to do the painting a second time in another color that my
first thought was, "Oh no! Not Again!"

At Bay

Acrylic on illustration board.
Copyright © 1984 by David A. Cherry.

At Bay stands as a rather unusual piece among my works. It was not privately commissioned, never appeared as a book cover, and compositionally was never designed to be a gallery piece. Around the time I first decided I wanted to actively seek cover assignments, it occurred to me that if I expected art directors to realize I could do cover paintings, I had to show them paintings which at least looked as though they had been designed for that purpose. With that in mind, I set about organizing a portfolio. This was my first painting for the portfolio, and in preparing it, I imagined that I had been given a cover assignment and approached the work with that in mind. It is fairly simple and straight-forward but has most of the elements I was seeking. It is bright and colorful (is certainly not green), with action and attention focused on a central figure, all with the top third of the work left open for title and type.

Back for a Friend

Painting for the cover of the role playing game
Fez I, *published by Mayfair Games, Inc.,*
Chicago, Illinois. Acrylic and oils on masonite.
Copyright© 1984 by David A. Cherry.

At the World Science Fiction Convention held in Los Angeles in 1984, I ran into a friend, Bill Fawcett, who was at that time with Mayfair Games, Inc. I was telling him about some new painting techniques I was anxious to try as soon as I got home. They must have sounded good because he immediately commissioned me to do the cover painting which became *Back for a Friend.*

I haven't done many paintings of dragons, but I do enjoy working on them when the opportunity presents itself. Dragons have existed in myth and religion since before the dawn of recorded history, and in all this time we have managed to imagine them as being of every possible size, shape, temperament, and moral creed. As a result, dragons provide fantasy artists with extremely fertile ground for the seeds of their imagination.

Here, I was primarily concerned with expressing the sheer brute power of the creature, but in the angle of the head, the turn of the mouth, and the expression in the eyes I tried to hint at sentience, the element which makes dragons such marvelous adversaries in so many fairy tales.

Esmeralda's Dance

Acrylic and oils on masonite.
Copyright© 1985 by David A. Cherry.

Esmeralda's Dance was inspired by the gypsy heroine of *The Hunchback of Notre Dame.* I do not care much for the heroines whose only contribution to a plot is that they stumble blindly into trouble and helplessly await rescue. Esmeralda, however, while she did require rescue, was portrayed as a character of great depth and dimension. Her inflexible faith in basic values, despite the pressures of a corrupt world which threatened her life, led ultimately to victory and, along the way, exhibited a strength of character which I find wholly admirable.

Still, in painting her, I chose not to portray her during her trials or in captivity but rather to envision her at her best, dancing alone in the forest at night for the sheer joy of it, free, at peace with herself and in communion with the world around her. In her exultation I found not only innocence, but a good deal of wisdom.

The Renaissance Man

Acrylic and oils on masonite.
Copyright© 1984 by David A. Cherry. In the
collection of Pat and Lee Killough.

The Renaissance Man is a fantasy portrait of friend and fellow attorney, H. P. (Pat) Killough, commissioned as a Christmas present by his wife, science fiction author Lee Killough.

Portraits are a very risky business: no matter how closely you feel you have captured the image of the subject, the person commissioning the portrait may disagree. I was very worried about this one. My only available photo reference was hardly larger than wallet size and showed Pat in a T-shirt, wearing thick-rimmed glasses which literally hid his eyes. Since the painting was to be a surprise, I could not ask him to pose personally or have new photos made. I had to rely on memory and imagination quite a bit. I had my fingers crossed until Lee and Pat called to give me the word: they liked it. Whew! Thank goodness.

Adveni

*Acrylic and oils on masonite.
Copyright© 1986 by David A. Cherry.
In the collection of Richard Kelly.*

In high school I studied Latin and ancient history. I was even an active member of our local chapter of the Junior Classical League. In college I studied Greek, classical art and archeology, Greek and Roman history, and majored in Latin. From time to time, elements of these studies pop up in my artwork, especially when, as in *Adveni*, I am working purely for my own self-expression.

All elements of the painting are authentically Roman, even the title which, in Latin, means "Come hither" (a reference to the young lady's beckoning glance). The challenge of the painting was to employ large areas of rather lifeless black and white in balance with areas of warm tones to create an environment which, as a whole, would come alive.

The most fun part of the painting for me was the aging of the wall painting. The wall was originally painted as a solid section, top to bottom. Then I sanded the areas where the wall painting would go, taking it back down to the gesso, leaving it just a bit dirty. Then I painted in the outlines of the figures with burnt umber and lightly stained the colors into the outlines. It was an experiment. I was surprised when it worked so well.

Keeper of the Vines

Acrylic and oils on masonite.
Copyright© 1985 by David A. Cherry.

Keeper of the Vines is one work where I consciously tried to achieve photographic realism. My concern was with the figure, the play of light and shadow on it, and I wanted little which would distract from that; so, instead of an elaborate background, I chose the simplicity of a wall. For perversity's sake, I elected to do the figure in blues (which tend to recede) to see whether I could make it stand forward against a wall of predominantly warm reds (which, themselves, tend to come forward).

I do not always want photorealism in my works. I do want to be familiar enough with my media to achieve it when I want it. If I choose to express myself through a rendering which is less than photorealistic, I want it to be a matter of artistic choice, not because my skills are so undeveloped that I am without a choice.

Daydreamer

*Acrylic and oils on masonite.
Copyright© 1985 by David A. Cherry. In the
collection of Gary and Pam Heath.*

The title of this painting is descriptive not
only of the central figure in the painting but
of my mental state as I created the work.
The scene is entirely from my imagination
and is typical of the places I like to visit in my
daydreams. Actually, it is only typical of
places I like to look at in my daydreams. If I
were to visit this little castle in the sky, I
would be forced to ruin the ambience by
installing elevators. The stairs would kill me.

I designed this painting not only to suit my
mood at the time but also to suit a particular
piece of photographic reference I had of the
model. The perspective was interesting, and I
did quite like the angle of the head as well as
her rather dreamlike expression, but what
really fascinated me were her hands. They
seemed to me to be in such an unnatural
position and yet, in their very unnaturalness,
gave such a feeling of quiet repose and ease.

Scattered Reflections

Acrylic and oils on masonite.
Copyright© 1984 by David A. Cherry.

Any artist has favorites among his paintings. *Scattered Reflections* is one of mine. My feelings for the piece are not based on any judgment as to the quality of the artwork itself. It is just one of those paintings which makes me feel good every time I look at it. Perhaps I am recalling the good mood I was in when I worked on it. I do recall having to struggle with it and repaint the figure even after I had once pronounced it finished. Perhaps I am merely recalling a sense of achievement at having overcome a difficulty. Mostly, though, I think I just love the grace and composure of the lady.

In this work you see my classical background slipping in again. The wall painting of flying fish is a reconstruction of a remnant of a Cretan fresco from Phylakopi in Melos, the original of which is estimated to have been done around 1550 to 1450 B.C. The girl, obviously not of the upper classes in garb or aspect, is, perhaps, a servant caught in an idle moment.

Man of Prophecy

*Acrylic and oils on masonite.
Copyright © 1984 by David A. Cherry. In the
collection of Lily Schneiderman.*

Sometimes the magic works. That is one
of my favorite sayings. Of course, that
means that sometimes it doesn't. But with
Man of Prophecy it did.

Unlike *Scattered Reflections* which I allow
myself to enjoy for rather nebulous reasons, I
am pleased with *Man of Prophecy* both aesthe-
tically and technically, and that is a rarity.

The background is an Assyrian relief
(from Iviz circa 750 B.C.—Aramaean-Hittite
style), though raised to gigantic proportions.
Its battered surface speaks of kings and
worldly power grown old and brittle. Before
it stands one man of no great wealth but
worthy and powerful in aspect, dwarfed by
the wall but self-reliant and confident in
his day and in his vision. In many ways
the figure speaks well for what I feel man
should be.

The Enchantress

*Acrylic and oils on masonite.
Copyright© 1984 by David A. Cherry. In the
collection of Muff and Real Musgrave.*

Like *Man of Prophecy, The Enchantress* also
portrays vision. This is fitting since they are
companion pieces...even more so since the
respective models are husband and wife.
Those of you familiar with the eminent
fantasy artist, Real Musgrave, and his brilliant and beautiful partner, Muff, may
recognize my good friends in these works.

As Real became an eloquent spokesman
for so many of the better qualities of
mankind in general, so Muff led me to
portray much that I find admirable in
women specifically. Certainly there is beauty.
Against a moderately ornate background,
the Enchantress herself is the only true
element of beauty. Her pose is passive, yet
that is but a pose. She is alert and purposeful,
yet patient and full of grace. In her hands she
holds magic, vision, and knowledge. Her gaze
is measuring, wise, and self-confident, her
smile enticing and full of mystery. In the
nobility of woman I find such enchantment
and more.

La Belle Dame du Rocher

Acrylic and oils on masonite.
Copyright© 1985 by David A. Cherry. In the
collection of Warren W. Chamberlin.

From one enchantress we turn to another,
La Belle Dame du Rocher—The Beautiful
Lady of the Rocks. This piece speaks of
darker mysteries but in so doing imparts a
moral lesson.

In literature and legend there are many
Belle Dames, each a siren possessed of
unsurpassed beauty but inhuman and soul-
less in nature. On foggy nights, the mes-
merizing lure of their song floats across the
waves to so excite the desires of men that, in
their headlong rush to embrace the Lady,
they sail instead to their deaths against the
rocks. The stories are not an indictment of
women. They are, rather, a warning to all
against the attractions of beauty for beauty's
sake without regard for the warmth and
goodness of the human soul.

The Offering

*Acrylic and oils on masonite.
Copyright © 1986 by David A. Cherry. In the
collection of Stanley and Beverley Hainer.*

My initial sketch for *The Offering* came
about almost by accident. I was visiting my
friends the Musgraves on an evening when
Real was supposed to be working on his own
paintings. I was afraid Muff would throw me
out if, as usual, Real and I spent the whole
evening talking, so I mumbled some excuse
about having a drawing I had to do (a white
lie), settled myself on the couch with my
sketchbook, put on the headphones to my
cassette player, and cranked up the volume
on some good ol' rock and roll. Real, unable
to talk to me, went back to work, and I,
feeling I had to come up with something to
justify my story, began to draw without any
idea as to what I was doing. I was just
relaxing into the music and letting my
thoughts flow out through my fingers into
images on the paper. *The Offering* is the result.

Soror Marium

Acrylic and oils on masonite.
Copyright© 1987 by David A. Cherry.

Soror Marium. In Latin it means Sister of the Sea. As with *The Offering*, this is a piece where I worked with no more reference than my own interests and imagination. In that sense, the work is extremely self-indulgent. Still, it has seemed to excite a good deal of interest and attention whenever I have exhibited it. That pleases me a great deal. As an artist, I find no greater joy than to work solely to please myself and find that I have touched my audience as well. At that point, the line between work and play has simply ceased to exist. I feel that something of what I see and am trying to express is being understood, maybe even appreciated. Communication, when it happens, is worth the effort it takes. When it happens without effort, the satisfaction for the artist is tremendous.

Twilight's Kingdoms

Cover of the book by Nancy Asire, published by Baen Books, New York, New York. Acrylic on masonite. Copyright© 1986 by David A. Cherry.

The first time I displayed work in an art show was in Kansas City in 1980. I was nervous and a bit embarrassed at the time, so a friend, Nancy Asire, was nice enough to assure me that the work was not all *that* bad. In fact, she said, she saw promise in it and would not be surprised if before too long I found myself doing illustrations and covers for science fiction and fantasy stories. She confided that she was, herself, an aspiring writer of fantasy. I recall her saying, "Wouldn't it be great if someday you could do the cover for my first book?"

At the time it all seemed an impossible dream. So, imagine my surprise in the Fall of 1986 when, shortly after learning that Nancy had sold her first novel, I received a call from Baen Books asking whether I would be interested in doing the cover.

Twilight's Kingdoms is the cover painting for Nancy's novel of the same title and is, in a very real sense, the union of two dreams.

I thought you might enjoy seeing some of the permutations a painting may go through on its way to becoming a cover. On the opposite page is the painting as originally conceived and submitted. Top right is an intermediate stage, the first requested alteration. Bottom right is the final version as used for the cover. The intermediate stage photo shows a wizard in the sky. The final version shows a dagger thrust into the burning city.

Shadowspawn

Cover painting for Thieves' World® Graphics *compilation Volume One, edited by Robert L. Asprin and Lynn Abbey, published by The Donning Company, Norfolk, Virginia. Acrylic and oils on masonite. Copyright© 1986 by David A. Cherry. In the collection of Robert L. Asprin and Lynn Abbey.*

Not too surprisingly, illustration is most enjoyable when the subject is a story you like. I am a big fan of the *Thieves' World* series and chose Hanse, one of my favorite characters, to grace this cover. For those girls who have asked to meet my model for this one, I am sorry. Hanse, at least this image of him, came straight from my imagination.

Actually, I must have come fairly close with the likeness. I received a personal letter from Hanse (typed but hand signed—he has just learned to print his name and is inordinately proud of his newfound ability) by way of Haldeman, Kentucky, saying that he enjoyed the portrait despite the fact that I show him with rather longish hair and holding his knife righthanded.

I know Hanse is sinister, but any good knife fighter is ambidextrous to some degree. And, hey, anyone can need a haircut now and then; so please, no letters of correction from the purists in the audience.

For those of you interested in technique, I might mention that this painting shows another application of the technique used to age the background fresco in *Adveni.* To achieve the weathered stone and plaster buildings, I painted layers of yellows, reds, and browns over a toothy gessoed surface, then sanded it back to the gesso. All I had to do after that was stain in the shadows and paint in the fine details.

Sanctuary

Painting for the back cover of the Thieves' World® Graphics *compilation* Volume One, *edited by Robert L. Asprin and Lynn Abbey, published by The Donning Company, Norfolk, Virginia. Acrylic on masonite. Copyright © 1986 by David A. Cherry.*

Night scenes are fun and a welcome change from the bright colors and flash of most cover assignments. On this back cover, the goals were to provide a contrast to the front cover (the brightly lit scene in *Shadowspawn*) yet maintain an air of old world charm and mystery, while providing an open rectangle to set off several paragraphs of type, all in about half my normal working time. A night scene centered on a shadowed doorway seemed my immediate best choice. I worked quickly, bringing my lights up from a solid dark ground. To speed my efforts, I chose a simple straight-on view with no tricky perspectives to work out. I love the way this turned out. Sometimes simple and fast is best.

The Last True Knight

Cover painting for The Last Knight of Albion *by Peter Hanrady, published by New Infinities Productions, Inc., Lake Geneva, Wisconsin. Acrylic on masonite. Copyright© 1987 by David A. Cherry.*

The Last True Knight is my first cover for New Infinities Productions. Just who is the last true knight? That bit of ambiguity in the title is intentional.

Certainly, the scene has an Arthurian flavor. The old man in the hood is easily identifiable as Merlin, so the knight, no doubt, must be Arthur. If that is your interpretation, I cannot say you are wrong. I will not, however, say you are necessarily right.

Insofar as the painting's use for the cover of *The Last Knight of Albion* is concerned, the old man is not Merlin. He is, rather, Arthur's own son, Mordred, now an old man living in obscurity as a hermit. The knight is Sir Percival, one of Arthur's youngest knights, now grown to manhood. Peter Hanrady's story of their interaction adds another fine chapter to the legends of Camelot.

Yet, the painting stands on its own merits apart from its use as a cover and tells its own story. Chivalry has supposedly been outmoded in this day of corporate ethics and pragmatism, but the images of Arthurian legend still speak to our conscience, reminding us of the value of more selfless aspirations. Who is the last true knight? I like to think that he has yet to be born.

Astronomical and Science Fiction Art

Orion Nebula

Acrylic on illustration board.
Copyright © 1983 by David A. Cherry. In the
collection of Judith R. Conly.

I am not well known as an astronomical artist, but at least two of my favorite works are of astronomical subjects. One is my painting of the Orion Nebula.

Nebulae are such beautiful works of art in themselves. It is easy to imagine God as an artist working the heavens as His canvas, first in the abstract forms of gas clouds and nebulae, then more tightly to the impressionistic images of stars, and finally more tightly still to the finely realistic details of satellites and planets. If so, the Orion Nebula is surely one of His master works. And I have always enjoyed drawing my inspiration from the masters.

I spent more time on this single painting than any I have done before or since. I did not want a painting of a photo. But I did not have access to a telescope of sufficient power to have my model "sit" for me. So, I studied every available photograph of the nebula for the uniqueness of its depiction and painted a synthesis of the images.

One day I would love a chance to see the original.

Crab Nebula

Acrylic on illustration board.
Copyright © 1984 by David A. Cherry. In the
collection of James and Ruth Shepherd.

My other favorite astronomical painting is also of a nebula, the Crab Nebula. Again, I worked from a variety of photographs, some in color, some black and white. I have always enjoyed those representations of the nebula as being of greenish hues and chose to represent it that way myself.

The painting of a nebula is much like attempting to do an accurate portrait of a piece of modern art. What went together so beautifully by chance in the original is hard to recreate faithfully. Just when you think you have the intricacies of a given section worked out, you look again and find that the section is out of proportion to the whole. It demands a great deal of patience, but the end result is well worth the time and effort.

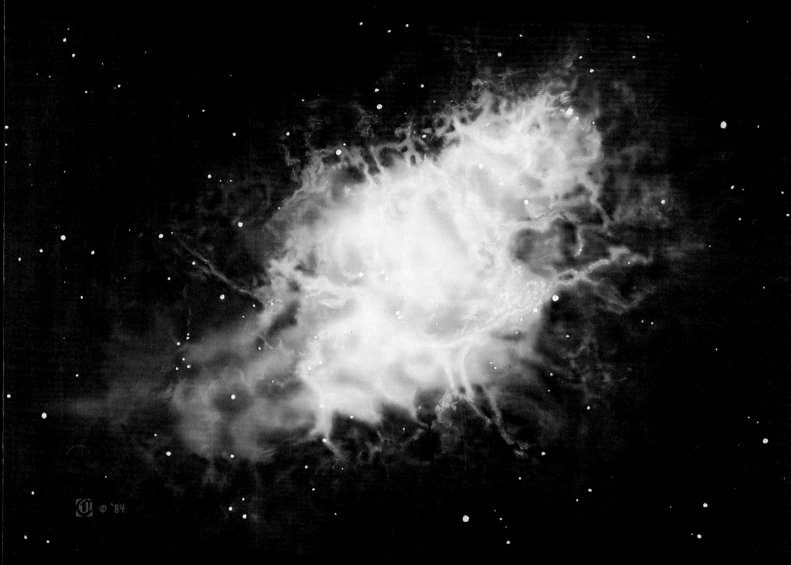

Trifid Nebula

Acrylic on illustration board.
Copyright© 1983 by David A. Cherry.

I had originally planned to paint the Trifid Nebula purely as an astronomical piece. This was, however, around the time I was preparing my portfolio to solicit science fiction illustration assignments, and I realized that while any decent portfolio of such type should contain paintings of spacecraft, I had none. In fact, I had never drawn a spacecraft before. So, combining artistic urge and artistic necessity, I came up with my own painting of the Trifid Nebula and my first interstellar craft.

Startide Rising

Painting for the wraparound dust jacket of the book by David Brin, published by Phantasia Press, Inc., West Bloomfield, Michigan. Acrylic on masonite. Copyright© 1985 by David A. Cherry. In the collection of Sidney Altus.

When Alex Berman of Phantasia Press offered me the assignment for the cover of David Brin's Nebula Award winning novel, *Startide Rising*, I was thrilled. I am an avid reader of Brin's fictional works and had greatly enjoyed that novel in particular. My mind was full of images of the neo-dolphin crew of *The Streaker* on the water world, Kithrup. I was, therefore, a little surprised to learn that the cover was to be of a more astronomical nature. In truth, I doubted the wisdom of the choice at first since so little of the actual story takes place in space, but the more I worked with the design potential of the scene, the more enthused I became with the idea. My only real restriction was that the scene took place in the vicinity of a gas giant, much like Jupiter, so I was totally free to turn my imagination loose with everything else. I loved it.

The Streakers Crew

Painting for the frontispiece of the David Brin novel Startide Rising, *published by Phantasia Press, Inc., West Bloomfield, Michigan. Acrylic on masonite. Copyright© 1985 by David A. Cherry*

In this painting I finally got to do a scene using the main characters from *Startide Rising*. Since virtually all of them are dolphins, I had to do a bit of research to be sure that I came as close as possible to an accurate portrayal of them.

In this scene you see three dolphin types. The three farthest to the right are of the species *Tursiops*. The odd one center-left is a *Stenos*. And coming in from above left is the evil hybrid of the story, K'tha-Jon.

For an artist, any experience is apt to be grist for the mill. Here I drew upon my memories of a vacation spent snorkeling off the island of Eleuthera in the Bahamas.

Vernean Voyager

Acrylic on illustration board.
Copyright © 1984 by David A. Cherry.

It was a fellow artist and friend, Hap Henriksen, who suggested the idea for *Vernean Voyager*. I had been trying to think of something fun to do for an upcoming art show, Hap suggested I try something whimsical as a change of pace. More specifically, he said he had always wanted to see what Jules Verne might use in the way of a space ship to take family and friends touring among the stars. I liked the idea and agreed to give it a try. In no time at all, Hap had me hip-deep in reference books from his extensive collection of turn-of-the-century "rocket ship" designs. *Vernean Voyager* is the result.

Here we see Mr. Verne's touring yacht deep in the reaches of the unknown. If you look closely, you may be able to see him in the aft salon entertaining guests.

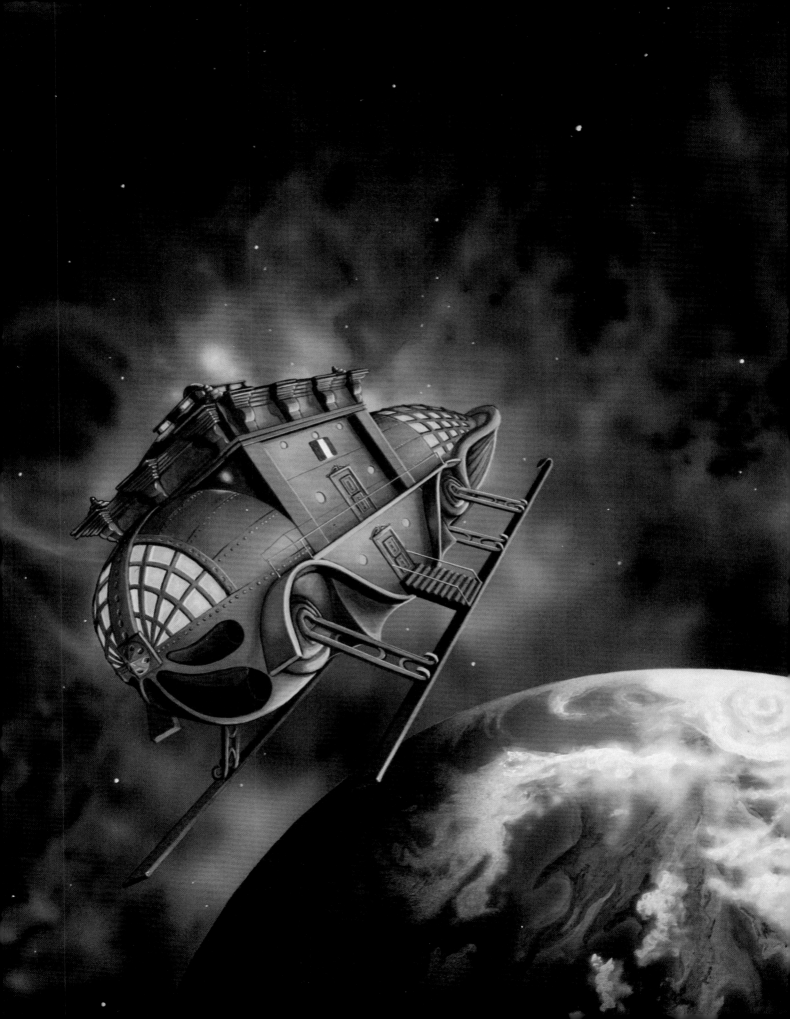

Lucy at Pell

*Acrylic on illustration board.
Copyright © 1984 by David A. Cherry. In the
collection of George D. Kramer.*

This painting was privately commissioned
to show the ship *Lucy* from the C. J. Cherryh
novel *Merchanter's Luck* coming in to dock
at Pell Station. Already at dock is a larger
merchant vessel of the *Dublin* class, dwarfing
poor battered old *Lucy*. Although it has never
been documented in any of her novels,
Carolyn assures me that the remnants of a
supernova are clearly visible in the starfield
surrounding Pell Station.

Quitting Time at Station Core

Acrylic and oils on illustration board.
Copyright © 1986 by David A. Cherry.

Quitting Time at Station Core is one of those strange paintings which evolved as I went along. I began the painting solely for my own amusement as an experiment in perspective. Before long I had this painting of a view down the central shaft of an orbiting space station sitting around the house. It was nice but not very interesting on its own. It needed people to add interest and give it scale. Unfortunately, I had been so interested in working out the perspective of the view that I had totally neglected to plan for any people in the scene.

Being the central core of a space station, the shaft would, of course, be a weightless environment. Where could I possibly put any people now that I wanted them? If I were to assume the spin of the station sufficient to provide enough gravity for anyone to walk around in the shaft (a dubious prospect in itself), I would have to paint their feet on the far walls with their heads toward the center of the shaft. That would present its own problems in perspective and would place the people so far away they would be too tiny to have any significant impact on the scene. Besides, I wondered, what would people be doing in there in the first place?

One morning I was daydreaming about the painting, and it hit me. Maintenance crews would have to work in the shaft. The area being weightless and very large, the crews would need maintenance carts to move them around. Now what sort of high-jinks would a crew like that get up to? I could see them at quitting time like water skiers in a null-gee race to see who would buy the beers. So, back to the drawing board for me, and this is what came out.

MAINTENANCE CART No.383

Voyager in Night

*Painting for the cover of the book by
C. J. Cherryh, published by DAW Books, Inc.,
New York, New York. Acrylic and oils on
masonite. Copyright © 1985 by David A. Cherry.
In the collection of William E. Shawcross.*

Voyager in Night is the cover of the DAW
Books reprint of Carolyn's book of the same
title. It was an interesting assignment to
undertake in that it required me to come up
with some way to represent a character who
is essentially a hologram and, hence, at least
partially transparent. In acrylic paint, this is
not a very easy thing to do. Even now I
would have to be very careful with the brush-
work, and at the time I really had no idea
how to tackle it effectively. My solution was
to do my background in acrylics and then
drybrush the figure in over that with oil
paints. All in all, I was very pleased with the
results, but I recall sweating it out all
through the underpainting, wondering
whether I would ruin it all at the end with
that troublesome figure.

Freight on Board

Painting for the wraparound dust jacket of the C. J. Cherryh novel, Pride of Chanur, *published by Phantasia Press, Inc., West Bloomfield, Michigan. Acrylic and oils on illustration board. Copyright© 1986 by David A. Cherry.*

I started to title this one simply F.O.B. Those who have read Carolyn's Chanur series will appreciate the humor of the title.

In this scene, the crew of the spacefaring merchant ship, *Pride of Chanur*, has just confronted an unwelcome intruder who has burst on board while they are at dock. Is it a sentient being or an animal? If it is sentient, it is certainly from an alien race never before encountered. What is it doing on board their ship? How dangerous is it? Where did it come from? And are more like this one on their way?

I may be prejudiced in my love of my sister's stories, but I cannot imagine anyone not enjoying the Chanur series. In four novels, she takes you not only deep into alien space but deep into alien mind-set and culture as well. You become involved not only in nonstop nail-biting excitement and suspense but in the history, economy, societal differences, politics and power plays of several alien races, all presented, not as humans in alien costumes, but as living, breathing, feeling beings, sensible in their actions but for motivations totally alien and totally intriguing. I am very proud of my sister for creating such marvelously detailed visions, and I am grateful I had the opportunity to be a part of their presentation.

Firefight on Kefk

Painting for the wraparound dust jacket of the C. J. Cherryh novel, The Kif Strike Back, *published by Phantasia Press, Inc., West Bloomfield, Michigan. Acrylic and oils on masonite. Copyright© 1985 by David A. Cherry. In the collection of Alex Berman.*

With their ship docked at a Kifish station far from their nearest allies or any hope of aid, the crew of *The Pride* grimly make their way past hordes of barely restrained Kif, trusting their lives to bluster and to a tenuous alliance with a renegade Kifish chieftain. Suddenly a shot blazes from the shadows. The corridors of the station erupt with civil war. And the Hani are caught in the middle. Again.

Firefight on Kefk was my first cover for Phantasia Press. The hardest part of the painting for me was figuring out how to handle the problems of perspective looking down the corridor of a huge space station. Just where do you put your vanishing points when the floor and ceiling curve up and out of sight? I wanted to be as accurate as possible, so I tried everything I could think of. I made models, took photos of them, worked out graphs and drawings, and even bought a text on vector analysis. In the end, I used the tried and true method. I eyeballed it.

To the Victor

*Painting for the frontispiece of the
C. J. Cherryh novel,* The Kif Strike Back, *published by Phantasia Press, Inc., West
Bloomfield, Michigan. Painting for the covers of
the editions of the same book published by DAW
Books, Inc., New York, New York and The
Science Fiction Book Club, New York, New York.
Acrylic and oils on masonite. Copyright© 1985
by David A. Cherry.*

I chose to illustrate this scene not only
because I appreciated its dramatic impact but
also because I had worked out all sorts of
sketches as to what the Kif looked like
beneath their robes and saw this fairly grisly
tableau as my one chance to present them
in a painting. It first appeared as the frontispiece to the Phantasia Press edition of *The Kif
Strike Back.* That was the only use I had in
mind for it. I was pleasantly surprised when
both DAW Books and The Science Fiction
Book Club picked up rights to use it for the
covers of their editions.

Chanur's Homecoming

Painting for the wraparound dust jacket of the novel by C. J. Cherryh, published by Phantasia Press, Inc., West Bloomfield, Michigan. Acrylic on masonite. Copyright © 1986 by David A. Cherry.

In this painting I was again faced with a scene in the interior of a space station. This time I was at least smart enough to avoid a view down the length of a station corridor.

Here, the forced alliance of Hani spacer clans desperately fight time and the politically immune Ehrran clan to retake Gaohn station in the face of impending attack by an incoming armada of alien warships capable of destroying not only the Hani station but their home world as well.

With some stories, it is difficult to find even one action sequence to illustrate. This can be a problem if you have an art director who is demanding an action scene on the cover, regardless. With the Chanur series, this was never a problem. Not only was I allowed almost total artistic freedom, but each story was so brimming with adventure that the only difficulty was in having to narrow my selection to one scene.

Apparently, I chose well on this one. It won the "Chesley" (the annual award of the Association of Science Fiction Artists) for best hardback book cover of 1986.

Chanur's Legacy

Painting for the frontispiece of the C. J. Cherryh novel, Chanur's Homecoming, *published by Phantasia Press, Inc., West Bloomfield, Michigan. Acrylic on masonite. Copyright © 1986 by David A. Cherry.*

Chanur's Legacy illustrates a scene at the very end of the Chanur series where a young Hani male, newly arrived on Gaohn station to begin training as a spacer, happens to meet a grizzled old veteran of the space lanes and gains a valuable insight into priorities and possibilities.

It would be very difficult to explain here why that scene means so much to me. You would have to read the entire Chanur series to appreciate its significance. Suffice it to say that, after reading it, I had tears in my eyes and wanted to stand up and cheer.

Sight Seer

Painting for the cover of the C. J. Cherryh anthology, Visible Light, *published by Phantasia Press, Inc., West Bloomfield, Michigan and by DAW Books, Inc., New York, New York. Acrylic and oils on masonite. Copyright© 1985 by David A. Cherry. In the collection of James and Ruth Shepherd.*

In her anthology, *Visible Light,* Carolyn used an unusual device to tie her stories together. She wrote herself in as one of the characters, a traveler to a distant star system who, during the voyage, tells tales (the various short stories) to a fellow passenger to pass the time and illustrate points of their continuing conversation.

This created the unusual opportunity to have the author appear on the cover as one of her own characters. A fun idea in itself, the fact that the portrait was to be of my own sister made it a real treat.

C. J. is seen conversing with a fellow passenger. The characters at left (forming the back cover) are from "Companions," one of the short stories in the anthology.

The version seen here is the full original work done for Phantasia Press. It appeared in slightly altered form in the paperback edition by DAW Books.

Visible Light

Cover of the audio tape and songbook,
Finity's End, *published by Off Centaur Press,
Albany, California. Acrylic and oils on masonite.
Copyright© 1985 by David A. Cherry.*

Visible Light is a study done for
consideration as the cover for the DAW
Books edition of Carolyn's anthology, *Visible
Light.* The objective was to come up with a
painting similar to *Sight Seer* in content but in
a format suitable to the dimensions of a
paperback cover, *Sight Seer* itself having
been designed for the entirely different
dimensions of the hardbound edition. It was
an interesting challenge, and I would be hard
put to decide which of the two versions I
like better.

Lady of Light

Acrylic and oils on illustration board.
Copyright © 1985 by David A. Cherry.

Before I was ever contacted by Phantasia Press about doing the cover for *Visible Light*, I was commissioned by DAW Books to do the cover for their edition. *Lady of Light* is the painting from the sketch originally approved by DAW's art director to be used as their cover for *Visible Light*.

I created the painting to be a striking design piece, and I believe it works quite effectively in that regard. I must admit, however, that the idea for it came by way of accident instead of design. I had done a pencil portrait of Carolyn on tracing paper, trying to work up ideas for the cover, but laid it aside to work on something else. When I looked for it again, I noticed I had placed it on the open page of a science magazine, right over a color photo of a series of particles streaming from a center of intense light. I did not think much of it at that time, but as I continued to work out other concepts for the cover, that image of the portrait super-imposed over the intense light source kept nagging at me, telling me it was much better than any of my carefully thought-out designs. Finally, I gave in and worked out the painting. It was ultimately rejected for use on the cover but has since won awards in several art shows.

Nova Satori

Painting for interior illustration of Robotech Art II, *published by The Donning Company, Norfolk, Virginia. Acrylic on illustration board. Copyright© 1987 by David A. Cherry. In the collection of Lynne Murray.*

In the Fall of 1986, Kay Reynolds, co-editor of *Robotech Art I* for The Donning Company, approached me with the prospect of doing an illustration for her next book in the series, *Robotech Art II.* The idea was for me to do a painting of one of the *Robotech* characters in my own style. Since the *Robotech* characters, although derived from superbly rendered Japanese animation, are essentially line drawings, highly stylized and presented with only a modicum of interior detail, the prospect of interpreting such a character in my realist style presented a considerable challenge. It was, however, a challenge which intrigued me and turned out to be a great deal of fun.

I was shamefully late in getting started on this painting. By the time I was ready, most of the book was already done. So, I asked Kay which characters had not been painted by other artists. To my delight, she felt a piece on Nova Satori would be good for the book. I really like Nova. She is not only attractive in a way which I felt comfortable interpreting in my style, but she is also one of the more interesting of the *Robotech* players. As usual with The Donning Company, I was given almost total freedom to create the painting as I saw fit. The combination of intriguing subject matter and artistic freedom helped a great deal in creating what turned out to be one of my favorite paintings.

Sublight EVA

Acrylic and alkyds on illustration board. Copyright © 1984 by David A. Cherry. In the collection of C. J. Cherryh.

According to scientific theory, if you go fast enough toward the speed of light, the visible star field will go chromatic, and you will be unable to perceive light along the axis of your movement. This creates an apparent hole in your vision of the star field, fore and aft, which grows the faster you travel, eventually reducing the star field to a chromatic band (or "starbow") which ultimately compresses to a single dimensionless white line of light as you actually attain the speed of light.

Imagine a ship with an enormous ramscoop in front to gather in and make use of such bits of interstellar matter as might otherwise hole the ship. It is already well on its way toward light speed, but repairs are needed on the exterior of the ship. In the glare of the ship's exterior lamps, a crew member emerges to effect the repairs. That is *Sublight EVA*.